THE HISTORY OF THE CHICAGO BEARS

Published by Creative Education

123 South Broad Street

Mankato, Minnesota 56001

Creative Education is an imprint of The Creative Company.

DESIGN AND PRODUCTION BY **EVANSDAY DESIGN**

LIBRARY OF CONGRESS CATALOGING-IN-PUBLICATION DATA

Frisch, Aaron.

The history of the Chicago Bears / by Aaron Frisch.

p. cm. — (NFL today)

Summary: Highlights the key personalities and memorable games in the history
of the professional football team nicknamed the "Monsters of the Midway."

ISBN 1-58341-291-3

1. Chicago Bears (Football team)—History—Juvenile literature. [1. Chicago Bears
(Football team)—History. 2. Football—History.] I. Title. II. Series.

GV956.C5F75 2004

796.332'64'0977311—dc22   2003063097

9 8 7 6 5 4 3 2

COVER PHOTO: linebacker Brian Urlacher

PHOTOGRAPHS BY

AP/Wide World Photos, Corbis (AFP, Bettmann, UPI/Corbis-Bettmann), Getty Images, Icon Sports Media Inc., SportsChrome USA

CHICAGO, ILLINOIS, WAS FOUNDED IN THE 1830S AS A SMALL GRAIN AND LIVESTOCK TRADING POST ALONG THE SHORE OF LAKE MICHIGAN. SINCE THAT TIME, EVERYTHING ABOUT CHICAGO HAS GOTTEN BIG. WITH ALMOST THREE MILLION PEOPLE, IT IS TODAY THE THIRD-LARGEST CITY IN THE UNITED STATES. ITS 110-STORY SEARS TOWER IS THE TALLEST BUILDING IN AMERICA. IT ALSO HAS BIG WINDS THAT BLOW IN OFF THE LAKE AND HOWL BETWEEN THE SKYSCRAPERS. THE PEOPLE OF CHICAGO ARE ALSO BIG ON PROFESSIONAL SPORTS. AND NO TEAM HAS ENJOYED MORE SUCCESS IN THE "WINDY CITY" THAN THE TOWN'S NATIONAL FOOTBALL LEAGUE (NFL) TEAM. AFTER SETTLING IN CHICAGO IN 1921 AND BEING NAMED THE BEARS—A NAME INTENDED TO TIE IN WITH THE CITY'S BELOVED CUBS BASEBALL TEAM—THE CLUB QUICKLY MADE ITS GROWL HEARD ACROSS THE NFL.

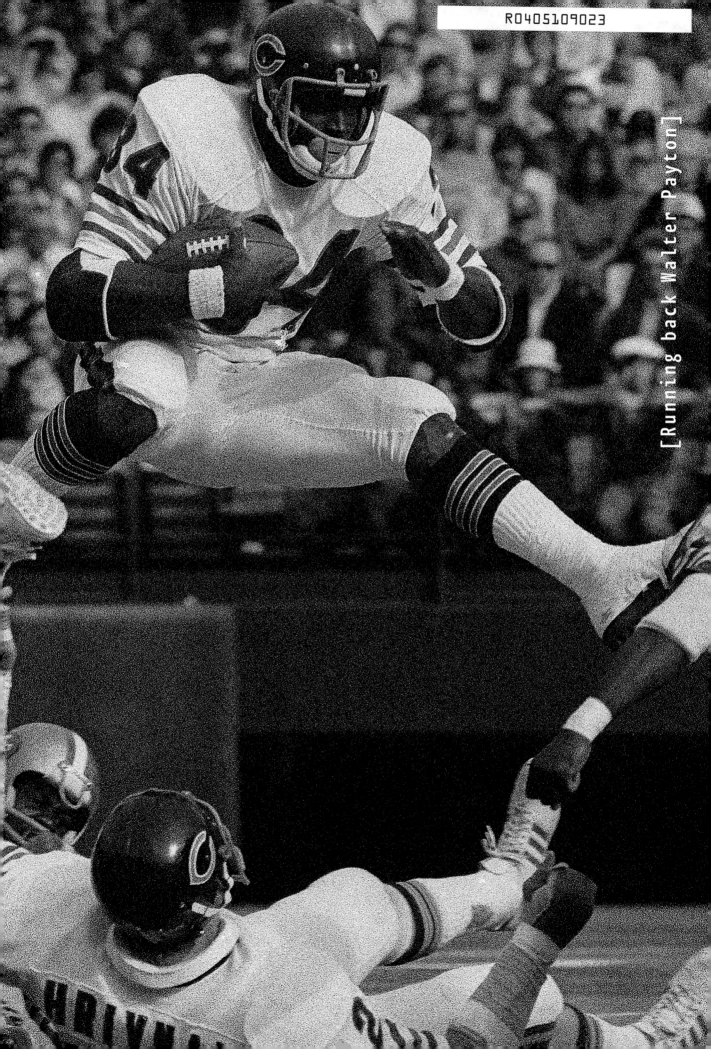

[Running back Walter Payton]

THE STORY OF the Chicago Bears begins with one man: George Halas. In 1921, when he was a 26-year-old athlete and businessman, Halas purchased a pro football team called the Staleys from the town of Decatur, Illinois. He moved the team to Chicago and soon renamed it the Bears. Halas, who would come to be known as "Papa Bear," would own the Chicago Bears for the next 62 years, also acting as coach for 40 of them.

Halas did a little bit of everything in the team's early years. He sold tickets, taped ankles, shoveled snow, coached, and occasionally put himself into games as an offensive end. He was also a football innovator and the first coach to schedule daily practices and study game films. Thanks to his efforts and those of such players as running back Ed "Dutch" Sternaman (a part-owner of the team), Chicago was an instant success, going 9–1–1 in 1921 and winning the league championship.

After playing for Chicago in the 1920s, George Halas coached the Bears in five different decades^

Halas ensured that the Bears would remain a powerhouse for some time by signing two exceptional running backs in the years that followed. The first was Red Grange, who joined the team as a rookie in 1925. In college, Grange had once run for 263 yards and four touchdowns in a single quarter, and his shifty running style earned him the nickname the "Galloping Ghost." Grange was the featured attraction as the Bears went on a famous 19-game cross-country tour in 66 days in 1925 and 1926.

Grange was joined in the Bears backfield in 1930 by fullback Bronislau Nagurski, better known as "Bronko." At 6-foot-2 and 230 pounds (a size considered enormous in those days), the former Minnesota farmboy was a punishing runner and a remarkably skilled passer, but he was perhaps most fearsome as a blocker paving the way for Grange. "When you hit him, it was like getting an electric shock," said Grange. "If you hit him above the ankles, you were likely to get yourself killed."

The Bears won two NFL championships in the 1930s. Chicago featured a number of great players during those years, including speedy running back Beattie Feathers and rough-and-tumble center George Trafton. But Grange and Nagurski were the heart of the team. The Bears won the 1932 championship game when Nagurski threw a short pass to Grange in the fourth quarter. A year later, Grange—playing as a defensive back—made a game-saving tackle at the end of the title game to make the Bears champs again.

BY THE END of the 1930s, age and injuries had caught up with the Galloping Ghost and Bronko Nagurski. Luckily, Halas found a new player who would keep Chicago flying high. That player was Sid Luckman, a talented college running back who was turned into a quarterback after joining the Bears in 1939. With Luckman and center Clyde Turner leading the offense, and with lightning-fast safety George McAfee (who was also a star runner and kick returner) sparking the defense, the Bears—nicknamed the "Monsters of the Midway"—went a stunning 37–5–1 from 1940 to 1943.

The Bears played some outstanding games during that stretch, but no performance came as close to perfection as the 1940 NFL championship game against the Washington Redskins. The Bears had lost to the Redskins 7–3 weeks earlier, and when the Bears complained about a controversial call, Redskins owner George Marshall called them

"quitters and a bunch of crybabies." In the title game, playing with pride and anger, Chicago destroyed Washington 73–0 in the most lopsided NFL game of all time. It got so bad that the referees eventually asked the Bears to stop kicking extra points. So many balls had been booted into the stands that the officials were running out of footballs.

The Bears remained a powerful team throughout the 1940s, winning the NFL championship again in 1941, 1943, and 1946. But after Luckman retired in 1951, Chicago no longer dominated. As always, the team had a number of terrific players. Running back Rick Casares excited fans with his Nagurski-like rushing style; Harlon Hill became the first Bears player to post more than 1,000 receiving yards in a season; and few players were tougher or more ill-tempered than linebacker Bill George and defensive end Ed Sprinkle. But from 1947 to 1962, the team made the NFL title game just twice, losing by wide margins both times.

A sense of normalcy finally returned to the Windy City in 1963. That year, behind a tough defense led by 6-foot-8 end Doug Atkins, the Bears went 11–1–2 and took on the New York Giants for the championship. The Giants had a great offense featuring running back Frank Gifford, but the Bears' defense was better. Chicago intercepted five passes and won 14–10 to capture its eighth NFL championship.

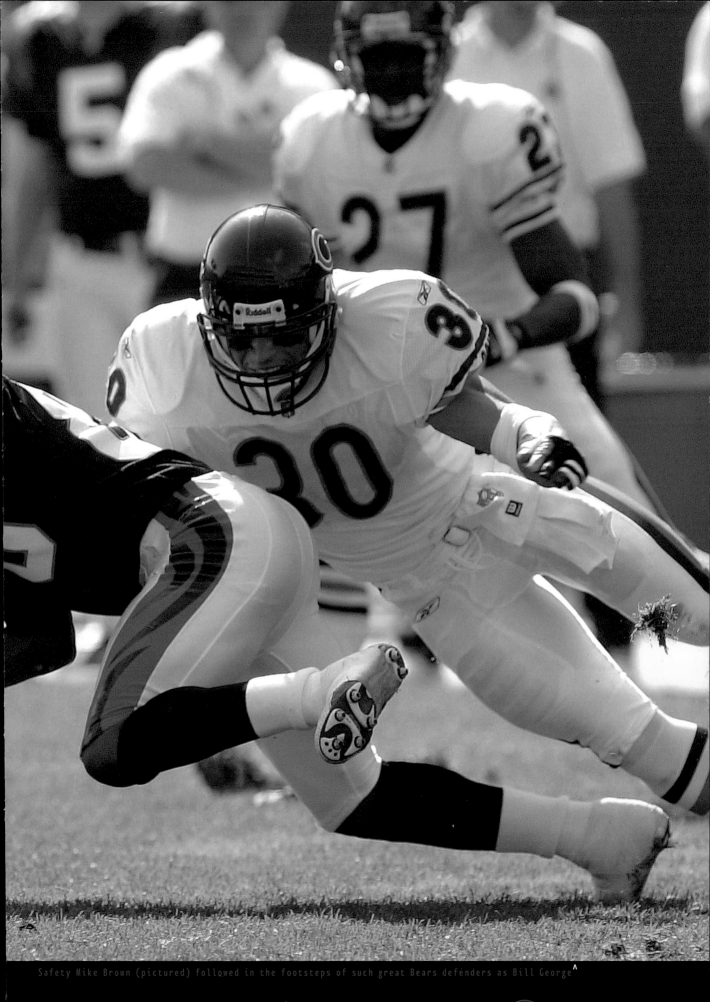

Safety Mike Brown (pictured) followed in the footsteps of such great Bears defenders as Bill George^

YEARS OF THE LEGENDS>

BEARS FANS DIDN'T know it yet, but 1963 was the last hurrah for a while in Chicago. Over the next 20 years, the Bears would put together just three winning seasons. The NFL was expanding to include more teams, and talent became more thinly spread throughout the league. Still, the Bears of the early 1960s were exciting to watch. They had two stars in Atkins and Mike Ditka—a hard-as-nails end who was both a sure-handed receiver and a devastating blocker—and in the 1965 NFL Draft they added two more: running back Gale Sayers and line-backer Dick Butkus.

An eight-time Pro Bowl selection, giant defensive end Doug Atkins was a one-man wrecking crew

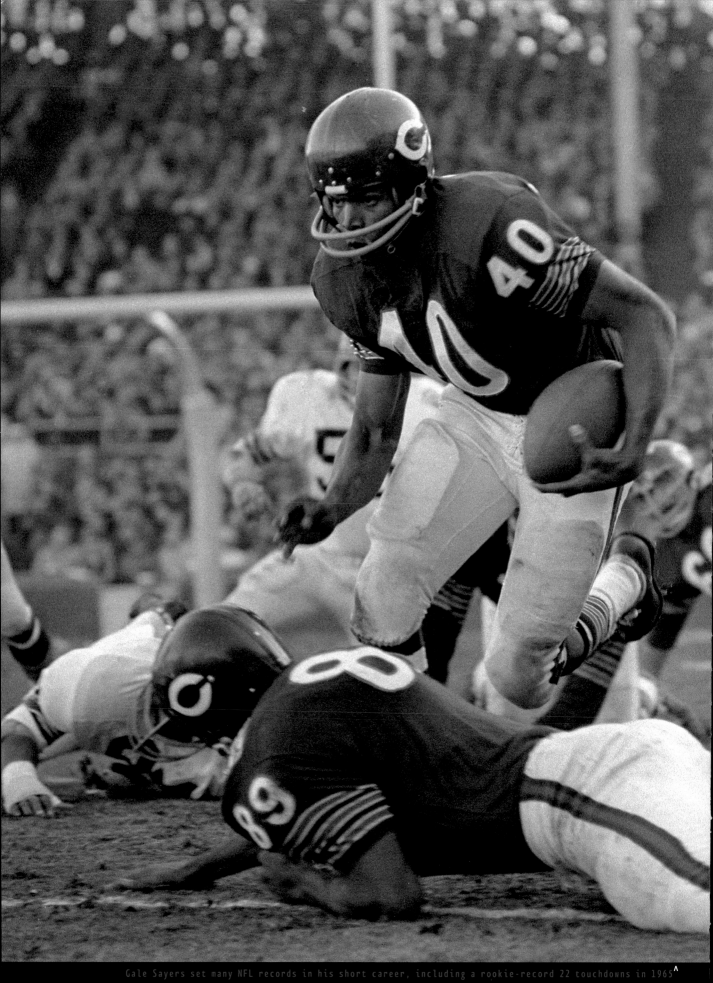

Gale Sayers set many NFL records in his short career, including a rookie-record 22 touchdowns in 1965

Equally spectacular as a rusher, receiver, and kick returner, Sayers was lightning on cleats. Fans and teammates would watch in amazement as he hurdled defenders and zigzagged clear across the field with his long stride. In one game against the San Francisco 49ers during his rookie season, Sayers scored an NFL-record six touchdowns—one on a pass, four on runs, and one on an 85-yard punt return. Sadly, his career spanned only six seasons before it was cut short by knee injuries.

While Sayers bewildered opponents, Butkus frightened them. Regarded by many as the most ferocious football player of all time, the 6-foot-3 and 245-pound linebacker played every snap with reckless abandon. Even though the Bears had a winning record only once during his nine-year career, he never stopped giving his all. "It's like he was from another world, another planet," Miami Dolphins guard Bob Kuechenberg later marveled. "He didn't run a [fast 40-yard dash], he wasn't a great weight lifter, but he just ate them alive, all those…sprinters and 500-pound bench pressers."

When Butkus retired after the 1973 season, fans had to wait just one year for the next Bears legend to emerge. That player was Walter Payton, a running back who as a kid had been more interested in band and gymnastics than football. Although Payton weighed just 200 pounds and was nicknamed "Sweetness," he was a classic Bears rusher who enjoyed running over—not around—defenders. Amazingly, in spite of his hard-nosed running style, he missed only one game in his 13-year career.

From 1976 to 1986, Payton rushed for more than 1,000 yards every season but one (only a players' strike in 1982 broke the streak). By the end of his playing days, Sweetness had carried the ball more times (3,838) for more yards (16,726) than any player in history. Perhaps the most amazing thing was that he did it despite the mediocre talent in Chicago during those years. As former San Diego Chargers tight end Kellen Winslow noted, "For most of his career, he took on the NFL with no offensive line."

A fiery competitor and savage hitter, Dick Butkus is widely considered the greatest linebacker ever.^

THE BEARS GROWL AGAIN>

IN 1982, 87-YEAR-OLD George Halas, who still owned the team, put the Bears in the hands of a new coach: former star end Mike Ditka. "Iron Mike" had earned a reputation as a tough guy during his playing days in the 1960s, and the fiery coach soon had the team on the rise. Behind the great play of Payton, young quarterback Jim McMahon, defensive end Dan Hampton, and linebacker Mike Singletary, the Bears went 8–8 in 1983 and 10–6 in 1984.

By 1985, the Bears were poised for greatness. Payton was as explosive as ever, and Chicago's defense—molded by feisty defensive coordinator Buddy Ryan—was the NFL's best. The Bears won their first 12 games in 1985 and finished with a 15–1 record. Defensive tackle Richard Dent led the NFL with 17 quarterback sacks, and the hard-hitting Singletary was named the league's Defensive Player of the Year.

Walter Payton became the NFL's all-time leading rusher in a 1984 game against the New Orleans Saints

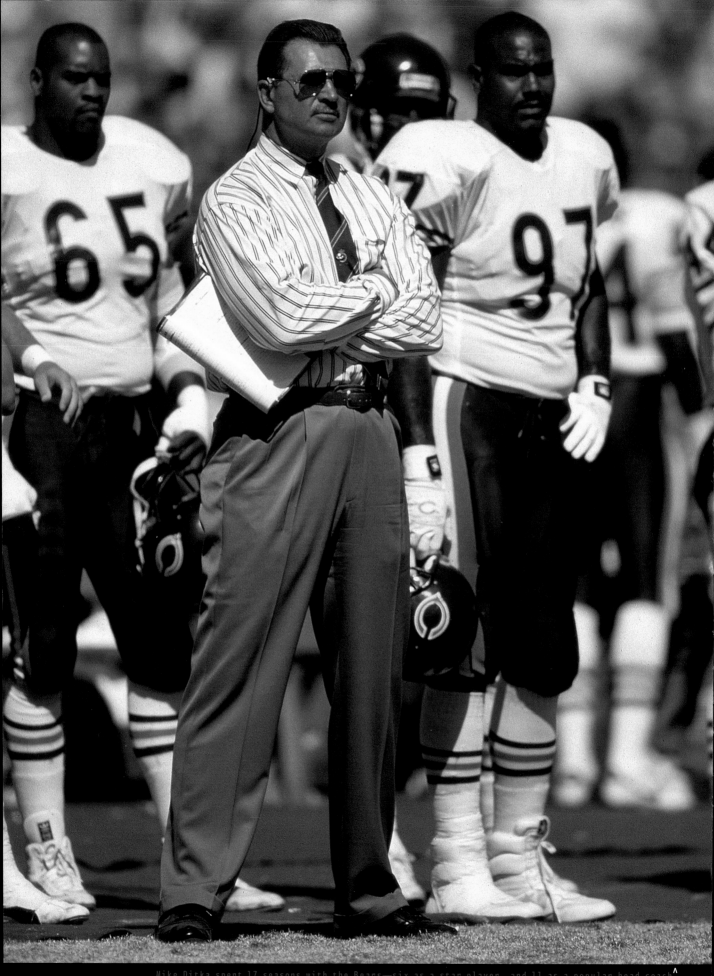

Mike Ditka spent 17 seasons with the Bears—six as a star player, and 11 as a popular head coach

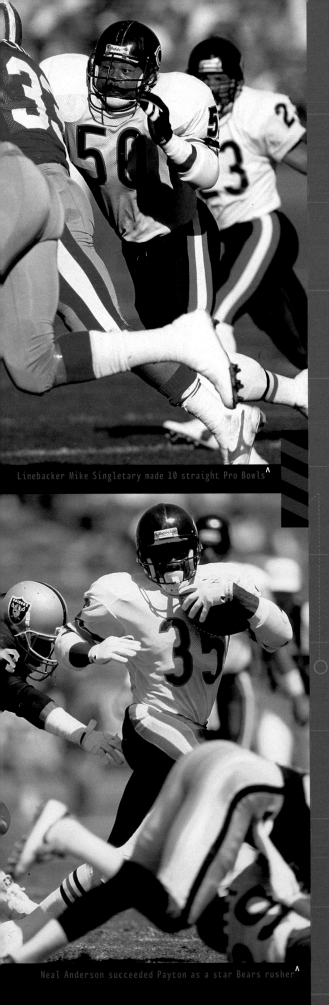

Linebacker Mike Singletary made 10 straight Pro Bowls^

Neal Anderson succeeded Payton as a star Bears rusher^

In the playoffs, the Bears were unstoppable. They crushed the New York Giants 21–0 and the Los Angeles Rams 24–0 to reach the Super Bowl. They then destroyed the New England Patriots 46–10 to capture the franchise's ninth world championship. "We've been working hard the last two years to be the best [defense] ever," said Dent after the victory. "I believe we're in the running. If we're not, I'd like to see who's better."

Chicago continued to dominate the National Football Conference (NFC) Central Division in the seasons that followed. Between 1984 and 1988, the Bears won 62 games—the most ever by any NFL team in a five-year span. They remained a league power through 1991 with the help of such additions as running back Neal Anderson (who replaced the retired Payton). Unfortunately, the Bears could not make it back to the Super Bowl. In 1992, after Chicago went just 5–11, Ditka stepped down as head coach.

WITH DITKA AND most of the stars of the 1980s gone, Chicago was a mediocre team for the rest of the '90s. The Bears seemed to have more than their share of bad luck during those years. Several promising young players—including running back Rashaan Salaam and quarterback Cade McNown—had short careers due to injuries or disappointing play after the Bears spent high draft picks on them.

In 2000, with head coach Dick Jauron at the helm, the Bears finally added the star they so desperately needed: linebacker Brian Urlacher. At 6-foot-4 and 260 pounds, Urlacher's size and skill (not to mention his crew cut hair style) had people comparing him to the great Butkus. In his first NFL season, he lived up to the hype by making 165 tackles and earning Defensive Rookie of the Year honors.

"It seems like he gets to places faster than anyone else," marveled Bears safety Mike Brown. "I've never seen someone so fast on the football field."

In 2001, the Bears ended their streak of losing football by putting together a surprising 13–3 record. Led by an aggressive defense headed by Urlacher and Brown, the Bears kept fans on the edge of their seats week after week, winning a number of games with frantic comebacks and trick plays. In back-to-back midseason games, the scrappy Bears came back late from 15 points down to the San Francisco 49ers and 14 points down to the Cleveland Browns to win both games in overtime on interception returns by Brown.

Although Chicago went just 4–12 and 7–9 the next two seasons, hopes remained high in the Windy City. In addition to its talented young defense, the team featured such rising offensive stars as quarterback Rex Grossman, receiver Marty Booker, and Anthony "A-Train" Thomas— a powerful running back who set a team rookie record with 1,183 rushing yards in 2001.

Since their start in Chicago in 1921, the Bears have put together a record of success unmatched by any team in NFL history. By 2004, Chicago had won nine league championships, and 26 team members—including Papa Bear George Halas—had achieved football immortality with induction into the Hall of Fame. Now, as they move into the 21st century, today's Bears are looking to become the Monsters of the Midway once again.

Marty Booker was a big, sure-handed target for Bears passers in the first seasons of the 21st century.

INDEX>